Swami Vivekananda

An Imprint of Om Books International

Published in 2015 by

An imprint of Om Books International

Corporate & Editorial Office
A 12, Sector 64, Noida 201 301
Uttar Pradesh, India
Phone: +91 120 477 4100
Email: editorial@ombooks.com
Website: www.ombooksinternational.com

Sales Office
107, Darya Ganj,
New Delhi 110 002, India
Phone: +91 11 4000 9000, 2326 3363, 2326 5303
Fax: +91 11 2327 8091
Email: sales@ombooks.com
Website: www.ombooks.com

Content by Shubhojit Sanyal
Illustrations by Aadil Khan, John Paulose, Sijo John, Himanshu Sharma

ISBN : 978-93-82607-72-4

Printed in India

10 9 8 7 6 5 4 3 2 1

Contents

The Early Years

Swami Vivekananda was born in a rich family on 12 January 1863 as Narendranath in Calcutta (now called Kolkata). His father, Vishwanath Datta, was an advocate at the Calcutta High Court, and his mother, Bhuvaneshwari Devi, was a pious housewife. The progressive, rational attitude of Narendra's father and the religious temperament of his mother helped shape his personality.

Narendra was spiritually inclined right from childhood. He was also an avid reader. He was greatly interested in ancient Hindu texts like the Vedas, Upanishads, Ramayana, Mahabharata, Bhagavad Gita and Puranas. Narendra was an all-rounder. He excelled in Indian classical music, sports and gymnastics. His range of knowledge was extensive and he loved to help people.

By the time Narendra completed his graduation from General Assembly's Institution (now Scottish Church College), University of Calcutta, he had acquired a vast knowledge of different subjects, especially Western philosophy and history. He had a yogic temperament and used to practice meditation. Some accounts say that Narendra had an impressive memory.

In Search of God

Ever since childhood, Narendra had great admiration for wandering monks and aspired to become one.

At the threshold of youth, Narendra passed through a period of spiritual crisis when he was confused about the existence of God. He began to search for scholars and spiritual leaders in order to question them.

But none of them could satisfy his curiosity. According to a legend, Narendra was first introduced to Indian mystic Ramakrishna Paramahamsa (the saint of Dakshineshwar) in a literature class given by William Hastie, the principal of his college. Narendra's meeting with the saint of Dakshineswar in 1881 proved to be a turning point in his life.

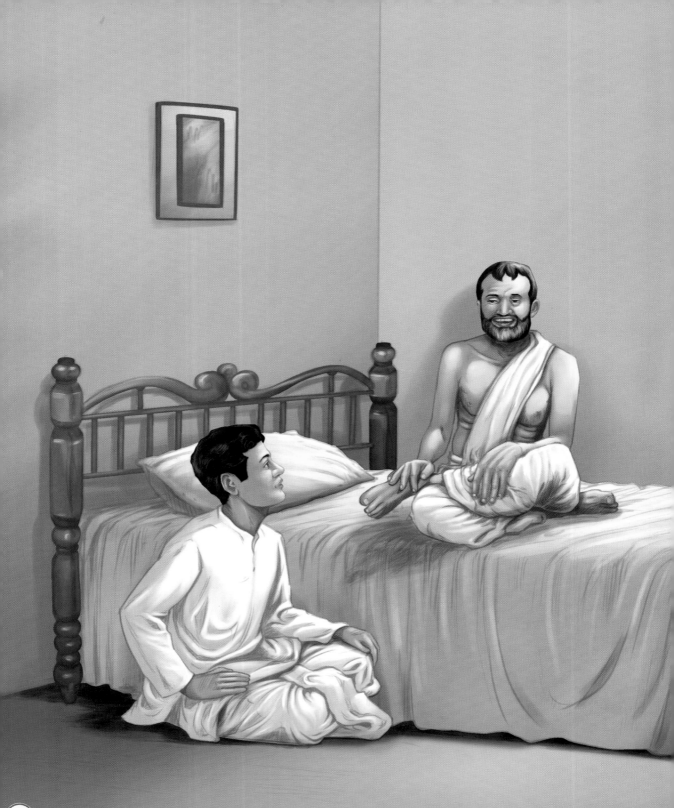

Personal Tragedies and Spiritual Light

When Narendra finally met Ramakrishna at Dakshineswar, he was very impressed with the saint. Although he did not initially accept Ramakrishna as his teacher and rebelled against his ideas, he was attracted to his personality and began to frequently visit him. As a member of Brahmo Samaj, he opposed idol worship and Ramakrishna's worship of Goddess Kali.

The sudden death of Narendra's father in 1884 left the family bankrupt. Suddenly, he became one of the poorest students in his college. He unsuccessfully tried to find work and questioned God's existence but found solace in Ramakrishna.

During this time, Ramakrishna was diagnosed with throat cancer. In September 1885, he was moved to a house at Shyampukur, and a few months later, to a rented villa at Cossipore, both in north Calcutta. In these two places, the young disciples nursed the Master with devoted care.

Ramakrishna instilled in these young men the spirit of renunciation and brotherly love for one another.

One day, he distributed ochre robes among them and sent them out to beg for food. In this way, Ramakrishna laid the foundation for a new monastic order. He gave specific instructions to Narendra about the formation of the new order.

Finally, on 16 August 1886, Ramakrishna passed away.

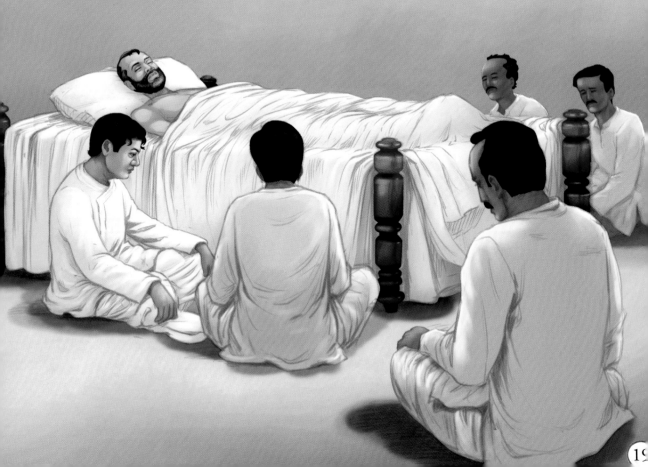

Establishment of Monastic Brotherhood

After Ramkrishna's death, his young disciples began to live together in a dilapidated building in Baranagar, north Calcutta, forming the Baranagar Math. Here, Narendra formed a new monastic brotherhood, and in 1887, all disciples took the formal vows of *sannyas*, thereby assuming new names. Narendra took the name of Swami Bibidishananda.

The disciples devoted themselves to spiritual practices intensely. Soon Swami Bibidishananda heard the inner call for a greater mission in his life. He received the blessings of Sarada Devi, wife of Ramakrishna, known to the world as the Holy Mother, and then renounced the world and travelled throughout India as a wandering monk.

In 1899, the Baranagar Math was shifted to Belur, and is now famously called Belur Math.

Travels across the Country

Swami Bibidishananda travelled far and wide through the extent of the country, visiting many holy places. He was deeply shocked to see the poverty and backwardness of the masses.

During these multiple travels, Swami Bibidishananda gained acquaintance of and stayed with scholars, dewans, rajas, government officials and people from all strata and walks of life — Hindus, Muslims, Christians and outcasts.

It was around this time (1893) that Swami Bibidishananda changed his name to Swami Vivekananda on the suggestion of his close friend and devoted disciple Maharaja Ajit Singh of Khetri.

Travels to Other Nations

During the course of his wanderings, Swami Vivekananda heard about the Parliament of World's Religions to be held in Chicago, USA, in 1893. His friends urged him to attend it.

Swamiji agreed to go on the trip after he got a divine call during his meditation on the rock-island at Kanyakumari.

Finally, with the funds partly collected by Swami Vivekananda's disciples from Madras (now called Chennai) and partly provided by the Maharaja of Khetri, Swami Vivekananda left for Chicago from Bombay (now Mumbai) in May 1893.

His journey took him through Japan, China and Canada, and he arrived at Chicago in July 1893.

Introducing India to the World

As soon as he arrived abroad, Swami Vivekananda learnt that he would need an endorsement from a known organisation. He felt isolated in the foreign land.

Taking pity on Swami Vivekananda, a lady provided him with food and shelter. On learning about his situation, she introduced

Swami Vivekananda to Professor John Henry Wright, who taught at the prestigious Harvard University.

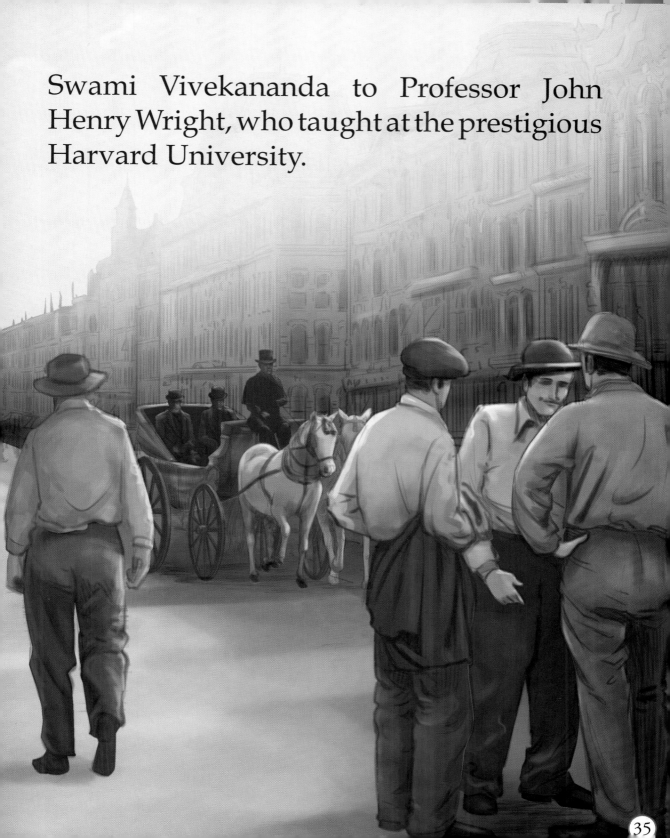

During his discussions with Swami Vivekananda, Professor Wright realised the true merit of Vivekananda's knowledge and he wrote a letter endorsing him.

Parliament of the World's Religions

Armed with Professor Wright's healthy endorsement, on 11 September 1893, Swami Vivekananda finally arrived at the Parliament of the World's Religions.

Swami Vivekananda created quite a sensation at the convention when he addressed the gathering as "sisters and brothers of America."

The entire audience rose to its feet and applauded hysterically for two minutes before some order was restored in the hall.

His speeches at the Parliament of World's Religions made him famous as an "orator by divine right" and as a "messenger of Indian wisdom to the Western world". Despite being a short speech, it voiced the spirit of the Parliament and its sense of universality.

He spoke several more times at the Parliament on topics related to Hinduism and Buddhism.

Growing Popularity and Appreciation

Swami Vivekananda gained almost instant popularity in the USA and was extensively covered by the newspapers. He was met with great appreciation and respect wherever he went.

Swami Vivekananda spent a good deal of time spreading messages about the holy Hindu scriptures as taught by Sri Ramakrishna in the USA and also in London. He established the Vedanta Society in New York in 1894.

In 1895, Swami Vivekananda travelled to England. He gained immense popularity there as well. There he met Margaret Elizabeth Noble, who later arrived in India and dedicated her life towards following the principles and teachings of Swami Vivekananda.

She spent the rest of her life educating women and helping in India's struggle for independence — she was more popularly known as Sister Nivedita, a name given by Swami Vivekananda.

In 1896, Swami Vivekananda travelled to England once again. This time he met the famous German indologist Max Müller, with whom he had several enlightening discussions about Hindu scriptures and philosophy. Both were very impressed with each other's knowledge. Their interaction culminated in a strong and lasting friendship. Swami Vivekananda finally returned to India in January 1897.

Swami Vivekananda first set off for Rameswaram in India and continued his journey towards Madras, and from there, to Calcutta.

From his spiritual discourses in the West, Swami Vivekananda then turned his attention towards the social inequality in India. He worked tirelessly towards removing poverty and the caste system, and also called for an end to British colonial rule over India. His speeches greatly influenced future leaders of the Indian independence movement, like Mahatma Gandhi, Bal Gangadhar Tilak and Netaji Subhas Chandra Bose.

The Ramakrishna Mission

By May 1897, Swami Vivekananda set up the Ramakrishna Mission in Calcutta; the following year, its headquarters was established in Belur Math. The Ramakrishna Mission undertook the teaching of Hindu philosophy and conducted various forms of social service like running hospitals, schools, colleges and hostels, in different parts of India and in other countries.

In spite of his failing health, Swami Vivekananda travelled to the West again in 1899, along with Sister Nivedita. During this period, he spent most of his time in the West Coast of the USA.

Swami Vivekananda's journey to the USA was very fruitful. He set up several Vedanta societies across San Francisco.

He also travelled to Paris, France, to attend the Congress of Religions in 1900. After delivering many lectures there, he returned to Belur Math in December 1900. The rest of his life was spent in India, inspiring and guiding people.

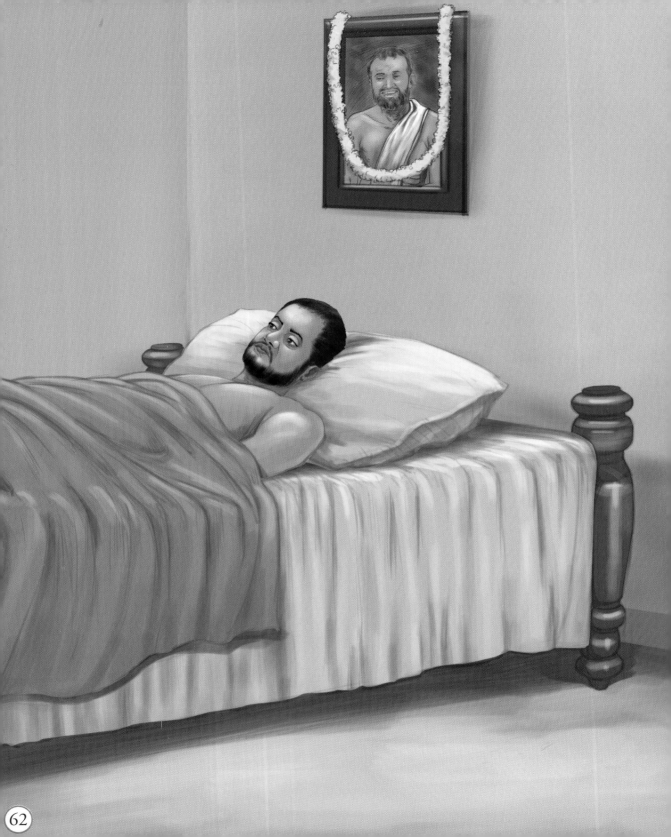

The Passing Away

Swami Vivekananda suffered terribly from asthma, diabetes, and chronic insomnia. He was a patient of various diseases and was also confined to his bed. He was a man of bad health and was invalid. Even in this condition, he tried to help people and lent a listening ear to all who needed him.

On 4 July 1902, after carrying out his duties for the day, Swami Vivekananda retired to his personal chamber and requested not to be disturbed. Shortly afterwards, he passed away following rupture of a blood vessel in the brain. He was not even 40 years of age.

Swami Vivekananda was cremated at Belur Math. Several Indian leaders and philosophers of the 20th century have acknowledged his influence. The great philosopher Sri Aurobindo regarded him as the one who awakened India spiritually. India's Father of the Nation, Mahatma Gandhi, counted him among the few Hindu reformers, who have maintained the Hindu religion by cutting down the deadwood of tradition. Netaji Subhash Chandra Bose rightly considered Swami Vivekananda to be "the maker of modern day India."

Rabindranath Tagore had once said, "If you want to know India, study Vivekananda. In him, everything is positive and nothing negative."

Ideals and Teachings

Swami Vivekananda's ideals continue to influence generations of people from all over the world. He is known to have written several books in his lifetime.

A few of Swami Vivekananda's teachings include:

One must give one's body, mind and speech for the welfare of the world.

The poor, the illiterate, the ignorant, the afflicted—let these be your God. Service to them is the highest religion.

Netiher money pays, nor name; neither fame pays, nor learning. It is love that pays; it is character that cleaves its way through hard walls of difficulties.

Don't play the blame game: Condemn none. If you can stretch out a helping hand, do so. If you cannot, fold your hands, bless your brothers and let them go their own way.

It's your outlook that matters: it is our own mental attitude, which makes the world what it is. Our thoughts shape things as beautiful, our thoughts shape things as ugly.

Be yourself: the greatest religion is to be true to your own nature. Have faith in yourselves!

No man is born to any religion; he has a religion in his own soul.

Man is not relegious by nature, but he is spritual. This helps him to understand the world and his fellow- beings better.

It is not easy to lead of fulfilling life, because the demand upon the soul are many. The man who understands this is able to grasp relegion, in its entireity.

Work unto death—I am with you, and when I am gone, my spirit will work with you.

We want the education by which character is formed, strength of mind is increased, the intellect is expanded and one can stand on one's own feet.

TITLES IN THIS SERIES

  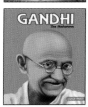 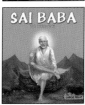 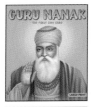 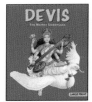

    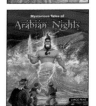